Awesome Adventures

Storybook with
Musical Microphone

Based on the series created by Michael Poryes and Rich Correll & Barry O'Brien

Contents

Reader's Digest
Children's Books®

Pleasantville, New York • Montréal, Québec • Bath, United Kingdom

Lilly, *Do You Want to Know* a Secret?

Quick! Lilly's coming! Turn me back into plain ole Miley!

Whoo hoo! I got 'em—two tickets to see Hannah Montana in concert!

Robby Stewart clicked off the TV with the remote. "Hear that, superstar? Hannah Montana: Sold out in Los Angeles."

"Woo-hoo!" his daughter Miley cheered. She struck a pose, modeling a new outfit. By day she was schoolgirl Miley Stewart, by night she was singing sensation Hannah Montana.

Suddenly, the phone rang. Miley answered it.

"Landing in twenty seconds," announced her best friend Lilly Truscott.

"Oh, great," said Miley, whipping off her wig. Quickly, Robby hid it in the piano.

Her brother Jackson took care of her jacket and glasses. "Sooner or later you're gonna have to tell her that you're Hannah Montana," he grumbled.

"Three seconds," said Robby.

"Two..." said Jackson, opening the door.

"One," said Miley.

Lilly sailed in airborne on her skateboard and skidded to a stop.

"Guess who just landed two tickets to the hottest concert in town?" asked Lilly. "You and I are going to see the one, the only, Hannah Montana!"

Yep, ketchup is a great moisturizer. Haven't you heard? Where you been?

"I don't get it," said Lilly as she and Miley carried their trays through the cafeteria. "Why won't you go to the concert with me?!"

They stopped at the condiment area for ketchup.

"I just can't go, okay?" said Miley.

Just then superjock Johnny Collins put down his tray next to her. "Hey, Miley, how's it going?" he asked.

Miley froze, then she started to speed-rap while pumping ketchup. It wasn't long before her hot dog—and hand—were covered.

As Johnny went to join some other jocks, Miley said, "He is so hot, and I am so lame."

You know, my hand DOES feel softer.

"Here's my lucky bracelet," Lilly said, taking it off and handing it to Miley. "Let's move."

Lilly nudged Miley toward the table where Johnny was talking to his friends. At that moment, Amber and Ashley slipped into the seats Miley and Lilly were about to take.

"Don't worry," said Ashley. "There are seats over there at the losers' table. Ooooh." Amber and Ashley touched fingers and made a sizzling sound. "Ssss."

Take it—it's my lucky bracelet. It never fails. Now go sit next to Johnny!

Miley! If you don't go with me to the concert, I'll have to go with "Mr. Montana" here.

"Okay," said Lilly as they sat down at the losers' table. "Minor setback. But the good news is...we have better seats for Hannah Montana!"

"I'm sorry, I...just don't like Hannah Montana," Miley said as their friend Oliver Oken sat down next to them.

Lilly opened her bag and pulled out a concert ticket.

"Miley, if you don't take this ticket, I'm going to end up going to the concert with Mr. Hannah Montana!" said Lilly.

"You have an extra ticket to Hannah Montana?!?" Oliver cried, and everyone on the quad came running over.

This is my life as Hannah Montana!

Miley walked into her house a total wreck.

"What happened?" Robby asked.

"Hannah Montana happened," Miley said.

"You mean the kids at school found out?" Robby asked.

"No, this was just about a concert ticket," Miley explained. "What if they found out I was Hannah Montana? No one would treat me the same."

"I bet Lilly would," said Robby.

"Are you kidding?" said Miley. "She's Hannah's biggest fan. If she knew the truth, I'd never be just Miley again.

This is the life! Hold on tight! And this is the dream, it's all I need!

That night at the concert the crowd was going wild. Hannah

Thank you, everyone!

You want my autograph? Funny, I'm not nervous at all when I'm Hannah.

Montana was decked out in her wig, sunglasses and long scarf, belting out a song. After the concert she stood in the doorway of her dressing room with a security guard and signed autographs. Johnny Collins stepped up.

"There you go," said Miley, handing Johnny his signed program.

"Thanks," he said, giving her a killer smile.

Robby, in his security guard disguise, closed the door. "Great show tonight," he said. "I'll go check the limo. Your mom would have been so proud of you."

"Thanks, Dad," said Miley.

"Higher, Oliver," said Lilly, hoisting herself up onto the ledge of Hannah's dressing room window. "I'm almost in."

"There is no higher," said Oliver. "You're already on my head!"

Lilly lost her balance and grabbed a light fixture hanging over the table. Accidentally she swung into the room, crashing into things.

Hey, it's Hannah Montana's dressing room. It's, it's, uh-oh!

It's not a pie, it's...um...a foaming facial pie. I mean, soap.

Hey! Your cellphone is ringing. Aren't you going to answer?

Miley came out of the bathroom, wiping her face with a towel. Lilly, too stunned to say anything, put a hand over her mouth, then started screaming, "Hannah Montana!"

Miley screamed, and Oliver lost his grip, crashing below.

Miley kept her back to Lilly. "Get out right now!" she said.

"Wait!" said Lilly. "I'm sorry, I was just looking for a souvenir. My name's Lilly Truscott and I'm a huge fan."

Miley grabbed a pie from the food table and shoved it into her own face. She lowered her voice. "It's not a real pie. It's a...foaming facial wash...pie."

"What's wrong with your voice?" asked Lilly.

"That happens after every concert," said Miley.

"I just wish Miley were here," Lilly said. "She's my best friend."

"Why don't you go get her?" Miley suggested.

"Great idea!" said Lilly, taking out her cell phone. "I'll call her!"

Miley's phone rang.

"Aren't you gonna get that?" asked Lilly.

"I'm talking to you," said Miley. "That would be rude."

Lilly waited for Miley to answer.

"Okay, she's not home," said Miley, snapping off Lilly's phone.

Miley's phone immediately stopped ringing.

Hannah Montana's towel! I'll never wash it!

"Why don't I just give you an autograph for her?" Miley said.

Oliver reappeared at the window. "What about me?" he asked. "I'm the one who loves you!"

"Take this towel," Miley said, throwing it to him.

"Hannah Montana's towel!" said Oliver blissfully.

"Well, I guess I'm leaving too..." said Lilly, "with nothing but my memories, which will fade too, too quickly."

"Here," said Miley, handing Lilly the scarf she'd worn on stage.

Why didn't you tell me, Miley? I mean, Hannah? Oh, I don't know WHO I mean.

"I have a lucky bracelet just like that," said Lilly, reaching for Miley's arm. "Of course mine says 'Lilly' on the back." She flipped the bracelet over. "Just like that."

The girls stared at each other. Then Lilly wiped some cream off Miley's face.

"Ta-da," said Miley.

The girls sat in silence. Lilly sulked sadly.

"Lilly, I know you're upset," said Miley. "But don't freeze me out. Talk to me."

Lilly, don't be mad. I'm sorry.

We're going to my closet because behind my closet is... my closet.

"I thought we told each other everything!" said Lilly, heading out into the hallway.

Miley followed close behind. "I wanted to tell you, it's just that I was afraid," said Miley.

"Afraid of what?" asked Lilly.

"I thought you'd like Hannah Montana more than you like me," said Miley.

Clothes. AND shoes. AND bags. Oh my!

"That could never happen, Miley," said Lilly. "Don't you know that?"

"Yeah, I do," said Miley. "No more secrets. I'm going to show you something!"

Miley opened the back wall of her closet, and there was a huge, brightly lit space filled with racks of outfits and shoes.

It's like a beautiful dream come true!

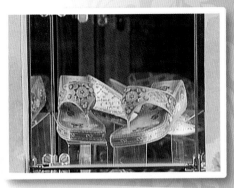

Okay, dream's over, I want those shoes!

"It's like a dream," said Lilly. "Okay, dream's over. I've got to have these." She grabbed a pair of shoes. "Wait until Amber and Ashley find out."

"No way! Once people know I'm Hannah, they won't treat me the same," Miley explained.

"That's the point!" Lilly said. "I'm talking mega-popularity here for both of us. Think about it. Johnny Collins would be so yours if he knew."

"No!" Miley cried.

Lilly accidentally banged her hand against the wall, hitting a button. The clothing rack started to move—and Lilly with it.

"How can you be so selfish?" Lilly asked. "If you were really my best friend you'd want this for me!"

She disappeared behind the clothes.

"And if you were really my best friend you'd understand why I can't do it!" Miley said.

"Come on, cut me some slack, Hannah," said Lilly.

"Hannah?!" Miley said.

Miley! I meant to call you Miley!

Let's never fight again!

Losers! Get out of our way!

Miley, are you thinking what I'm thinking?

Upset, Miley sat down on the revolving platform. "I knew this would happen," she said.

"Did I say Hannah?" said Lilly. "It was a mistake."

"No, the mistake was trusting you," said Miley.

"Wait, Miley, I'm sorry, but that was major news. You gotta give me a little time," said Lilly.

"What happens if you can't?" Miley asked. "What about the next time you get dissed by Amber and Ashley? Are you sure you won't want to tell them?"

"Of course I'll want to, but I won't," Lilly promised.

"Hugs?" the girls said together.

The next day at lunch on the school quad Amber and Ashley entertained other kids with stories about Hannah's concert. Miley, Lilly and Oliver walked by with their trays. Oliver wore the towel Hannah gave him around his neck.

"We were in the first row and—" Amber began.

"—Hannah smiled right at us," Ashley finished.

"Big deal," said Oliver. "See this towel? She gave it to me in her dressing room."

"You're pathetic. Oh..." said Amber and Ashley as they touched their index fingers together. "Ssss...."

"Wait a minute," Miley said to Amber and Ashley. "He's telling the truth. And she gave Lilly something,

How did THEY get Hannah's scarf?

Lilly, give 'em Hannah's scarf.
You'll be glad you did, I promise.

too." Miley pulled out the scarf from Lilly's bag, then hung it around Lilly's neck.

"That's Hannah Montana's scarf..." said Amber.

"Yeah. Hannah gave it to her," said Miley.

Lilly gave Miley a grateful smile. Then she said, "But you know what? You should have it." She put the scarf over Amber's shoulders. Ashley grabbed it.

Hey! Amber is wearing Hannah's scarf!

"It's Hannah Montana's scarf!" Miley and Lilly said together.

Everyone on the quad came running over to Amber and Ashley.

They were mobbed by the crowd! And Miley and Lilly touched fingers, "Ssss..."

Stampede!

Oooh. Ssss!

She's a
Super Sneak

Robby was in the kitchen cleaning a fish while Jackson watched, disgusted.

"So what's it gonna be Bucky, pan fried or barbequed?" asked Robby.

"Dad, remember what we said about naming the fish?" said Jackson. "It makes them a little harder to eat."

At that moment Miley came downstairs. "Dad, the new Ashton Kutcher movie is previewing tonight. Can I go?" asked Miley.

"Mile..." Robby began.

"I can go?" Miley asked hopefully.

"No, you can stop," said Robby. "You know you gotta study. And that goes for your brother too."

Pretty pleeeeze, Dad. I've just got to go see the new Ashton Kutcher movie.

Robby changed to go out. Then he handed Jackson a book. "You guys think I'm being too tough?"

"Yes," Jackson and Miley said at the same time.

"Good. That means I'm doing my job right. Study hard now," Robby said as he left the house.

Miley sighed, then got down to work. On the floor. On her stomach.

Time to crack the books!

Studying a la skateboard!

Textbooks make great helmets.

Jackson balanced a book on his head—and used a book as a headrest. Then he lifted his shirt and and painted a face on his stomach.

Miley yawned. "Wow," she said, checking the clock. "Eight minutes already."

"Yup," said Jackson's belly button-turned-mouth. "Time to turn in. Good thing I'm not an outie."

"Cover him up, we've got company," said Miley.

Miley opened the door. "Lilly, my dad said no," she told her friend.

"You think he said no, but he really said go," said Lilly. "Come on. I heard Ashton Kutcher's gonna be there."

"Now you're just being cruel. But that's good, it's workin'," said Miley.

"Okay, now all we gotta do is sneak you out without Jackson knowing," said Lilly.

After Lilly left, Miley went upstairs.

Jackson's phone rang. "What's up, Cooper?" he said.

His friend Cooper was calling from the theater where he worked as an usher. "Hey, check this out,"

Who says studying is boring?

Your dad didn't say "NO," Miley, he said "GO." They sound the same.

Jackson, you're missing an opportunity here.

Miley is such a goody-goody. She never does anything bad.

he said. "There is a very hot rumor that Mr. Ashton Kutcher is dropping by here tonight."

"I don't know, Coop," said Jackson. If I split, Miley's just gonna tell my dad. Of course, she is in her room."

Meanwhile Miley was climbing down a rope ladder hanging from the back window.

"You know what?" said Jackson. "She won't even know that I'm gone. I just talked me into it!"

Jackson dashed upstairs. A muffled scream came from Miley as the rope ladder came loose and fell.

The multiplex was filled with girls milling about. Jackson arrived and spotted Cooper.

"Cooper, you are a genius," said Jackson.

"Watch and learn," He spotted a pair of girls with their backs to him. "Prepare to be impressed."

Jackson started toward them. Cooper followed.

"So...Mr. Kutcher!" Jackson said into his phone.

The girls turned around. It was Miley and Lilly.

What are YOU doing here?

Don't tell Dad!

"Aaaaaahhh!" Jackson and Miley cried at the same time. "I'm telling Dad!"

"No, you're not," they both said.

"Because we're not really here right now," said Jackson.

"Right," said Miley. She gasped. "But Dad is."

Sure enough, outside the entrance to one of the theaters was Robby, eating popcorn and looking at a poster.

"What's he doing here?" Miley wondered, crouching behind a cardboard cut-out. "He said he had a meeting."

At that moment, Oliver came over. "Lilly? Miley?"

"Miley's dad's here," said Lilly.

"We've gotta get out of here," Miley said in a hushed tone.

Dad's here too! I thought he had a meeting.

Robby turned away and glanced at his watch.

"Wait, my bag," Miley said.

The friends moved the cut-out forward and Miley reached out and grabbed her purse.

Jackson's phone rang.

They peeked out from behind the cut-out and saw that Robby was on his phone.

"Don't answer it," said Miley. "Keep moving."

"I have to answer it," said Jackson. "He thinks we're at home."

"Hey, Dad! We're home!" Jackson said brightly into the phone.

"Studying at home! H.O.M.E.!" Miley added.

How long will we hide behind this sign?

Hi Dad! We're home. H.O.M.E. Home!

Wait a minute, who's that?

"I just called to check in on you guys. Whatever it is that you're doing that you don't want me to know you're doing, stop doing it. Bye," said Robby, hanging up.

Just then an attractive young woman entered the lobby and approached Robby. Then she took him by the arm and the two went into the theater.

"I don't believe it," said Miley.

"I know," said Jackson. "The old man can get a date and I can't!"

Back home in the kitchen, Miley paced, while Jackson sat at the table, eating a giant sandwich.

"Why did Dad go on a date and not tell us?" Miley asked.

"Miley, it's been three years. He's probably lonely," said Jackson.

"I hear him!" said Miley, heading for the door.

"Just play it cool," said Jackson.

Is there anything you'd like to tell us, Dad? Anything at all?

"Where have you been?! We agreed home by eleven. And it's..."

Robby checked his watch. "Eleven-o-three?"

Collecting herself, Miley said, "Right. How did your...um... meeting go?"

"Don't worry," said Robby. "If it keeps going the way it's going, I'll tell you all about it."

He gave Miley a kiss on the head and rubbed Jackson's hair affectionately, then headed upstairs. "Love you guys," Robby said. "Good night."

She's homeless and she sells homes? Weird.

Hey! Get out of my drawers!

"I can't believe we don't even know her name," said Miley.

"Movie Saturday night...Margo Diamond," Jackson read from Robby's PDA. "Hey, isn't she that lady from the real estate sign?"

"We've got to go to her office and check her out!" Miley cried.

"Alright, let's do this," Miley said, adjusting her Hannah wig.

Miley and Jackson walked over to Margo's desk.

Dad alert! And he's got flowers!

"I'm Hannah Montana, and I'm looking for a house," said Miley.

"What a thrill to meet you. My niece is a big fan of yours," Margo told Miley.

Miley looked up and saw Robby walk in, holding flowers. Miley and Jackson dropped to the ground.

"Ms. Diamond, excuse me and my chauffeur, we have to confer... in private," said Miley.

Miley and Jackson quickly ducked into a nearby closet.

Quick! In the closet!

Robby went over to Margo's desk with the flowers.

Hannah Montana is in my closet!

Uh-oh. Guess we're out of the closet.

"Hi," Robby said shyly. "I had a nice time last night."

"So did I," said Margo. She hung up the phone.

Inside the closet Miley and Jackson fought for space.

"I would love to go out for coffee," Margo told Robby. "Let me just get my coat." In a soft voice she added, "You're not going to believe this, but I've got Hannah Montana hiding in my closet."

"Huh?" said Robby. He went over to the closet. "All right, come on out...now," he said.

Miley slid open the closet door and glared at Robby.

"How could you try to replace Mom?" Miley said, fighting back tears as she stormed out.

Gee, Dad, thanks. I sure got lost!

How could you replace my mom?

Mom, I Miss You.

Why didn't you tell me?

Later that evening Miley picked at her guitar and sang part of a song called "I miss you".

Robby came out on the patio and listened until Miley noticed him and stopped.

"That's a beautiful song, honey," said Robby, sitting next to her. "I guess I was hoping to tell you at just the right time."

"I just can't picture you with anybody but Mom," said Miley.

"Neither can I," said Robby. "What she and I had was special."

"Then why are you dating?" asked Miley.

"Because life goes on. Don't you think your mom would've wanted that for us?" asked Robby.

Miley thought about it for a moment. "Yeah, I guess."

The two hugged.

"What's this rope ladder doing here?" Robby asked.

"Let's not ruin a beautiful moment," said Miley.

Honey, I'm sorry.

And we'll talk about this rope ladder real soon.